Eugene Mason

Flamma Vestalis

and other poems

Eugene Mason

Flamma Vestalis
and other poems

ISBN/EAN: 9783348063883

Printed in Europe, USA, Canada, Australia, Japan

Cover: Foto ©Andreas Hilbeck / pixelio.de

More available books at **www.hansebooks.com**

Flamma Vestalis

IN SAME SERIES.

The Lady from the Sea.

A London Plane Tree, and other Poems.

Iphigenia in Delphi.

Mireio.

Lyrics.

A Minor Poet.

Concerning Cats.

A Chaplet from the Greek Anthology.

The Countess Kathleen.

The Love Songs of Robert Burns.

Love Songs of Ireland.

Retrospect, and other Poems.

Brand.

Son of Don Juan.

Mariana.

Flamma Vestalis.

BY SIR E. BURNE-JONES.

Flamma Vestalis

AND OTHER POEMS

by

EUGENE MASON

CAMEO SERIES

T.Fisher Unwin PaternosterSq.
London E.C.   MDCCCXCV.

A. 90029

Contents.

	PAGE
For Burne-Jones' Flamma Vestalis .	7
A Love Duet	9
A Ballad of the Silver Hind . .	11
Ideal Love	20
My High Princess . . .	21
At Benediction .	22
The Nuptial Mass . .	23
The Blue Rose	24
The Rose Garden . .	25
For Burne-Jones' Dies Domini .	26
Giorgione's Kiss .	27
Biblia Pauperum . . .	28
Suggested by Perugino's Madonna and Child	30
Spiritual Art	32
In the National Gallery . . .	33
Art of Arts	34
From a Library Window .	36

6   CONTENTS.

	PAGE
Colombe's Birthday	38
Winter Evenings	40
For J. K. Huysman's " A Rebours "	41
After Reading " Mdlle. de Maupin "	42
Rossetti's Gift	44
Dante's Grief	45
In Memory of John Keats	47
A Woman's Hair	48
Prisoners of Hope	49
A Child's Dreams	51
The Dream Child	53
The Flower Bride	56
Raymond's Mistress	57
In Memory of David Gray	58
Death's Gifts	59
A Ballade of Proserpine	60
The Song of Her Body	62
A Spring Carol	65
Prelude to a St. Dorothy	67
Old French	69
Sonnet after Baudelaire	71
Exotic Perfume	73
An Old Goldsmith	74
The Chatelaine	75

For Burne-Jones'
Flamma Vestalis.

IN purple vestment, and in gathered hood,
 The Vestal Virgin passes down the
  street,
  With recollected thoughts, and covered
   feet,
And downcast eyes where folded memories
  brood.
No love hath stirred her bosom, no man
  wooed,
  She walks on ways with holy tasks replete,
  With half-told beads, and symbolled rai-
   ment meet,
A handmaid vowed to Vesta, white and good.

Ah, Love, foreknown, compact of hope and
  dream,
This painted ghost thy shadow as I deem,

To thee with beckoning hand and song
    I cried ;
Haste, love, and tend the lit lamps of thy
    shrine,
Warm breast and face at this red hearth of
    mine,
No Vestal, but a woman, and my Bride.

A Love Duet.

M^Y heart and I beguile the weary ways
   With dainty converse in our Lady's
      praise.

In sweet duet we find our Lady fair
From slim white foot to dark upgathered hair.

Who loves the more, nor heart nor I can tell,
So dear she is and so desirable.

Yet when I sing my Lady's mist-veiled eyes,
Her mouth made tremulous with low replies,

The ordered fashion of her simple dress,
The slender wonder of her loveliness,

My heart rebukes me, pleading I prefer
This outward show and vestiture to her.

For this my heart repeats in every place,
That she herself is fairer than her face,

And sweeter far than voice, or lips, or cheek,
The candid thought that bids her mouth to
     speak.

Thus loving one her body, one her soul,
My heart and I together love the whole ;

And ease the burden of life's heavy ways
With dainty tribute to our Lady's praise.

A Ballad of the Silver Hind.

" REST in my bower, dear Lord, to-day,
　　My soul is sick with fear,
My heart doth ache ; for Mary's sake
　　Chase not the silver deer.

" Six months ago for my maiden wreath
　　You gave me a golden crown,
And the bridal gift I got that tide
　　I bear beneath my gown."

" I cannot rest in thy bower, sweetheart,
　　Where the maidens sew and sing ;
To sit till night by the red fire-light
　　Would ill beseem a King."

" Last night I dreamed that I was dead
    And cold as any stone,
And a silver hind stood by my bed
    And bade my soul begone."

He caught the weeping Queen to his breast,
    He kissed her pallid mouth,
" Another dream you shall dream e'er morn,
    A fairer dream in sooth."

He waved his hand as he rode away,
    " Blow horns for the merry chase."
But the Queen's lips stirred with no farewell
       word,
    And hers was an ashen face.

With winded horn and baying hound,
    With knife and hunting spear,
He sought till noon before he found
    The slot of the silver deer.

The hind sprang forth from a leafy brake
    Where the weary hunter stood,
Like sudden snow, like bolt from bow
    She sped for the distant wood.

Her hoof was white as the silver bright,
    Like shining gold her horn,
Her body fair as a maiden's breast
    And sweet as springtide thorn.

With winded horn and baying hound,
    With knife and hunting spear,
O'er field, and hill, and forest glade,
Through mountain stream and dappled shade,
    He followed the silver deer.

With voice, and rein, and bloody spur
    He urged the swift steed on ;
The hounds drew close to the flying prey,
He gripped the knife in his lust to slay,
    When, lo, the hind was gone.

The hounds crept back like a whimpering
    child,
    The stout steed plunged and neighed,
The King's blood pricked like points of ice,
    So sore was he afraid.

He swore an oath and he crossed his breast,
    To Saint Hubert paid his vows,
And staring round, but a bow-shot off
    He marked a fair white house.

" A draught of wine for a weary man,"
　　He beat on the oaken door ;
An eldrich laugh rang down the hall
　　And a witch girl crossed the floor.

Her hair was red as the shining gold,
　　Like silver her naked feet,
Her body lithe as the leaping fawn,
　　Her breast as the whitethorn sweet.

Her gown was thin as the finest silk
　　And laced with a purple band,
A garland fair was about her hair,
　　A gold ring on her hand.

She poured the wine, and she pledged the
　　　　cup,
　　His cheek was of ruddy hue,
So fine were the folds of her silken vest
　　Her limbs showed whitely through.

She held the draught to his eager lips,
　　A leman to his mind,
He gazed o'er the wine to her subtle eyes
　　And knew the silver hind.

He sought her love as a wondrous thing,
   (God grant him shameful death),
" Thou hast a bride to thy bed, O King,"
   (The Queen's heart sickeneth).

" Give me the spousal ring from her hand,
    The circlet from her head,
      (List what the wise leech saith),
And thrust her forth to her father's land
    And crown me Queen in her stead."
      (The Queen swoons on to death.)

They wrapt the Queen in' her grass-green
    cloak,
   With a shroud o' the sendall white ;
Her maidens filled in the new-digged grave
   At dusk, by the red torch light.

Next morn where once was a fresh-digged
    grave
   They found a garden fair,
With grass as green as a grass-green cloak
   And tendrils curled like hair.

All pleasant flowers and smelling herbs
 Stood thick about that place,
Wet roses red as the Queen's true heart,
 Pale lilies like her face.

In a hidden spot where the leaves grew close
 A pool rose still and clear,
'Twas deep as the eyes of a six months bride,
 And a white bird fluttered near.

The King wed fast with that subtle witch,
 He loved her passing well ;
She prayed no prayer at the bridal mass,
 Nor knelt at the sacring bell.

In cloth of gold and cloth of silk
 They sought the banquet hall,
Betwixt her head and the staring sun
 Lords bore a crimson pall.

" What garden fair, my little page,
 Hath grown before my door ? "
" It grew last night from my lady's grave,
 It ne'er was seen before."

" Whence came this bird, my little page,
  That flutters there alone ? "
"O that, my lord, is your dead Queen's soul,
  She makes a weary moan."

The witch sped fast to that painful bird,
  Her face was drawn and wan,
She gave her many a bitter word,
  " I bid thy soul begone."

The white bird passed like a little cloud,
  The flowers hung faint and wan,
The garden shrunk to a new-made grave,
  The Queen's fair soul was gone.

The witch bride held with charm and spell
  Her groom in silken bower,
Such wondrous love did king ne'er prove
  For dame nor paramour.

The dead Queen's kith for their sister's wrong
  Harried with torch and sword ;
She crooned in his ear a magic song,
  He marked no other word.

The poor folk clamoured at his gate,
　　Lean, ragged, nowise fed,
They marked his sloth, his pomp of state,
　　His luxury of bread.

They cried, " See how these wantons fare,
　　They lie on down and furs ;
We snatch our victuals from the dogs,
　　We kennel with the curs."

One morn they burst the gilded gates
　　With weapons grim and rude,
They plucked the King from his leman's arms
　　And slew him where he stood.

They mocked his brows with a tinsel crown,
　　They filled his mouth with chaff,
But the rudest stayed in his bloody toil
　　To hear the witch bride laugh.

She fled through the crowd of the gaping
　　　　men,
　　She gleamed down the burning street,
Her golden hair was stained with fire,
　　Blood stained her silver feet.

She passed to the haunts of the foolish men
    With the spell of her subtle eyes,
Her breast is a snare, and her fallen hair,
    And her mouth of wine and lies.

Woe to that man who is lured by her face
    And her specious words and kind,
He shall break his heart in the headlong
        chase,
His soul shall pass quick to its destined place,
    For the love of the silver hind.

Ideal Love.

A S one who passes from the busy street
    Within the hush of some religious place,
    May kneel awhile upon the altar-pace,
And pray, forgetful of the noise and heat.
He hears the fall of unscen angel feet,
        Faint incense odours breathe against his
            face,
        And where the tapers light a little space
He sees the pictured Mother, sad and sweet.

So in my heart I have a chapel fair
        For Love to pray in, hid from common
            stir,
        Enriched by music, dim with burning
            myrrh,
But all the worship, all this glow of prayer
        Are hers to whom dear love doth minister,
A slender girl, pure-eyed, with gold brown hair.

My High Princess.

AS midst the jewelled throng some high
     princess
  Might pass unwitting of her father's thrall,
  Moving with gracious laughter down the
     hall,
Shod with red silk, and tired with pearl
     decked tress—
He marks the dainty fashion of her dress,
  Her bright flushed face, her foot's rose-
     softened fall,
  The perfume, and the blaze of festival,
And all the love that serves her loveliness.

He dare not choose but worship,—not as one
  Who craves for guerdon,—what may his
     deep shame
  Possess in common with her stately name !
Yet though his ways may never know the sun,
Though but a slave whose summer hours
     seem run,
  Deep in his soul is kindled love's white
     flame.

At Benediction.

SHE knelt beneath the flaming central light,
    Whereon was wrought Maid Mary in her
        cell
    Heark'ning   the   cold   high   words   of
        Gabriel,
Who bore three Lady-lilies, tall and white.
My love's bowed face was hidden out of sight
    In tender palms, and on her bright hair
        fell
    Faint stains of crimson, whilst the organ's
        swell
Shook the hushed church in pauses of the
        Rite.

The dusk drew down, the gold and purple
        went,
    Yet still she knelt,—ah, surely not in vain
    Was   that   dear   prayer,   but   from   the
        darkened pane
To hear her words the Virgin Mother bent,
    Whilst on her soul was shed, like silver
        rain,
The Benediction of the Sacrament.

The Nuptial Mass.

THE chancel glows like Paradise above—
 Glorious with gold to shadow forth
  Christ's Bride,
 Gleaming with lights to hail the Crucified,
Fragrant, to speak the unction of the Dove.
Surely His Banner over us is Love,
 As knit for ever, kneeling side by side
 In prostrate worship of the Lamb Who
  died,
We break that Bread the world knows
  nothing of.

Love, I am all unworthy thus to gain
 Your gracious gift of spotless womanhood,
 About you Raphael's guardian angels
  brood,
 And how dare I profane their sweet
  control ;
For should your stainless soul from mine take
  stain
 Surely my soul must answer for your soul.

The Blue Rose.

I HEDGED and tended my strict garden
        close,
    I rid the soil of each infructuose weed,
    In patient hope I gave my plot good heed
Through autumn languor, and the winter
        snows.
In pain and tears, with more than woman's
        throes,
        I strewed the ground with myth and
            dream for seed,
        Watered with brooding mists of many a
            creed,
So I might raise one magical Blue Rose.

And now that summer's gold is nearly done
    I know my garden but for barren sand,
    Enchanted blossoms fail the naked land,
And in the chill warmth of a sunken sun
I pluck the single prize my toil hath won,
        This spray of withered hedge flowers in
            my hand.

The Rose Garden.

ONCE in my dreams I found an ivory house
    Gardened with rose and vine-leaf for a
      screen,
      Wherein a maid walked reading, grave
        of mien,
Whose Eastern eyes knew well the coming
      spouse.
Then one ran softly, flushed by holy vows,
      Who closed the painted hours of Mary,
        Queen,
      And led his bride across the petalled
        green
To love's own home, and ent'ring, kissed her
      brows.

Ah, God ! the sunshine shivered off the close,
      Music and colour fled the darkened day,
      My dream wailed low, with golden face
        turned grey,
And as it passed a winter's wind arose,
The garden whitened under sudden snows,
      And I,—I crossed my breast and turned
      away.

B

For Burne-Jones' Dies Domini.

LORD, not in terrors, not with falling stars,
  Eclipse, and moaning sea, and quaking
      earth,
  Despair, division, monstrous things at
      birth,
Loud war, and flying rumour of loud wars.
Think rather, Christ, upon Thy piteous scars,
  Remember not our sins, our little worth,
  Or then indeed would Hell enlarge her
      girth,
And cheerless laughter shake her molten bars.

Come, Lord, on angel pinions, grave and calm,
  Ringed round with tender face, and
      flame-crowned head,
  Their raiment blue as hope, yet plumed
      with red,
And bearing in Thy raised and wounded palm
Healing and consolation, oil and balm,
  Divine Physician of the quick and dead.

Giorgione's Kiss.

THIS man the gods loved blindly ; moon
 and sun
 And stars bowed down before him. Each
  good thing,
 —Fame's rustling raiment white and
  glistering,
A presence maidens turned to gaze upon—
Became his portion, and his work was done
 In shadowed gardens where the women
  sing,
 By marbled wells whence mirroring
  waters spring,
Near sea-wed Venice, noiseless as a nun.

And lest his years should sink with sad eclipse
 In dull senescence, grudging, lost to praise,
 Ere youth and love withdrew their
  golden haze,
They broke life's thread with piteous finger
  tips,
 And gave him in the shortness of his days
Death, caught like perfume from his lady's
  lips.

Biblia Pauperum.

(ST. MARY THE VIRGIN.)

SERVANTS of Mary they, and dear to God,
  Who wrought this painted scripture of
    His spouse,
  This cloistral girlhood hid within God's
    house,
The mystic bridegroom with the lilied rod.
Or one fraught hour when Gabriel's feet,
    flame-shod,
    Bore the swift Ave, and her sevenfold
      woes,
    Till clothed in flesh, Christ's circlet on
      her brows,
Free from the festal grave Heaven's courts
    are trod.

Star of the Sea—when white the surge, and
    wild,
    And hidden fears grow instant, and
      revealed,
    If self itself prove recreant and would
      yield,
In that dread tide, O Fountain undefiled,
    Fast Ivory Tower, O Garden fenced and
      sealed,
Mother of God, remember me, thy child.

Suggested by Perugino's Madonna and Child.

CHOKED, barren, blind, the desert
        stretches wild,
    The haunt of robber band, and hidden
        slaves,
  With sultry wastes one winding river laves,
Where no bird sings, and never flower has
        smiled.
Yet here are fled the Mother and her Child,
    And Mary kneels adoring him she saves
    From Herod's fear, and with pure praying
        craves
God's pity on the weak and undefiled.

Mark well the answer. Sky and dreary sand
    Burgeon to life with cohorts of the Lord,
    Michael stands girded with the flaming
        sword,

Raphael who led Tobias by the hand
Now guides these Pilgrims, yea, all under-
ꞋꞋ   stand
As hand to lip Christ signs " I am the Word."

Spiritual Art.

WITHIN the hush of some tree-hidden
    bower,
    Beneath the sombre breaking of the day,
    In soft dead grace Eve's tender body lay
Till God gave spirit to complete her dower.
Then burst the opening bud to perfect flower,
    Then flesh woke manifest from senseless
        clay,
    Then voice, and life, and movement,
        marked the sway
Of some divine impenetrating power.

So in these latter days our English art
    Like mother Eve lay fair yet deathly
        numb,
    Till God's own breath aroused her from
        the trance,
    And—giving speech to her who yet was
        dumb—
Mated to outward grace the better part
    The soul of rich and high significance.

In the National Gallery.

A SQUARE with fountains, slopes of steps,
  a hall,
  And then the magic of this jarring room ;
  Here, pallid Christs adored within a tomb,
There, the White King, or whirling Bacchanal.
Here scourge and vigil hold the flesh as thrall,
    There Venus smiles, rose-crowned, with
      burthened womb,
    Or women struggle in the ravished
      gloom
Whilst lusty life keeps riotous carnival.

Is it indeed all well that here we praise
    Contending schools, and creeds that dwell
      apart !
We walk like wizards on divergent ways,
    But ah, we love not with the single
      heart,
Better, perchance, to build in temporal days
    Narrow, but deep, the channels of our art.

Art of Arts.

THIS is the land of make-believe and
masque,
Haunted by flute, and horn, and lilting
rhyme,
Where rhythmic feet pulse fast in ordered
time,
And gilt-haired dancers pose in languid task.
Romance moves here in plume and glancing
casque
Through dreams of dainty love, exotic
crime
Here dwells delight, with fool and
lacquered mime,
Or draped in purple wears the brazen mask.

Mirage and rainbow gold are ours to gain—
    A fairer world where art and song have
        strayed,
    Loves lovelier far than love of mortal
        maid,
Ideals fruition spoils not nor makes vain,
A faery place where weeping leaves no stain,
    And sorrow is but joy in masquerade.

From a Library Window.

THESE are the golden streets, whereon for
    gain
    Girls harshly laugh, and worn men flag
      and tire,
    Where whoso walks is spotted with the
      mire,
And hopes die down, and dreams are dreamed
    in vain.
Symbols of sickness, Hospital and Fane
    Speak soul and body passed through
      Moloch's fire,
    Whilst all sweeps blindly to the common
      pyre
And God keeps silence.—Leave the window
    pane.

Here life goes softly as before a shrine,
    These ways with children's tears are
        never wet,
    Things fair and lovely in this place are
        set,
Tristram and Yseult knit by flower and spine
Lie here, and deep mid daisied grasses shine
    The gleaming feet of moonlit Nicolette.

Colombe's Birthday.

THUS from my hair I pluck the coronet,
—My brow throbs easier now I lose its
      weight—
   Unclasp the brooch pin of this robe of
      state,
A year's mistake, please God, not life's regret.
Woman, not duchess—now I quite forget
   The empire Fortune carried as her
      freight,
   And simple maid choose simple man for
      mate,
So thou wilt wear me as love's amulet.

Give me your hand. You called me once
      "play queen,"
   Love is the priest, he crowns me ever
      thine,
   Anoints with sacred oil this head of
      mine,

Garbs me in cloth of gold with jewels sheen,
> Thrones me for good or ill, through rain
>> and shine,
Queen of thy soul, Colombe of Ravestein.

Winter Evenings.

WITH what keen joy I hear the clock
    strike five,
    For rising from my chair I drop the pen,
    And mixing with the crowd of passing
      men,
Swarm homewards, as a weary bee to hive.
I sometimes dream I am but half alive,
    Till, with the lamplight, in some cosy
      nook,
I feel the firewarmth on my cheek, and dive
    Within the pearl-strewn depths of some
      loved book.

For then I quite forget my poor estate,
    The hidden future, and my restless heart,
    And soul absorbed in some soft poet's
      page,
    Hear low-voiced damsels whispering
      apart,
Mark silken galleys laden with rich freight,
    And breathe the perfumes of another age.

For J. K. Huysman's
A Rebours.

WHENCE came this woman to our alien
   air !
   What sun-steeped lands, what teeming
      mines and seas
   Gave this rich gaud of fringed embroide-
      ries,
These lucid gems her gilded bosoms bear ?
She dwells in western towns, perversely fair,
   The fume of opium dreams within her
      eyes,
   Her body impregnate with essences,
And spotted, leprous orchids in her hair.

The taint of moist decay is on her breath,
The sense of wasting hours and fetid death,
   And in her proffered hand strange gifts
      she brings,
A palsied will, a heart's paralysis,
Satiety and loathing—these and this,
   A snake that turns upon itself and stings.

After reading " Mdlle. de Maupin."

YEA, though the carven work be fair and
   good,
   The arches shapely, and the rich shrine
      dim,
   Though through the silence steals a
      perfect hymn
And all be wrought in Art's divinest mood,
Yet think not that the goddess deigns to
      brood
   Above the altar reared and decked by
      him
   To whom the body's beauty, white and
      slim,
Is all the fair and true of womanhood.

A woman's love is other than you deem,
  And only those are worthy of the prize
    Who mate high living with a noble
      creed ;
    Who strive by self-control and tender
      deed
  To catch the spirit-love which never dies
When flesh is clean forgotten as a dream.

Rossetti's Gift.

A S the white soul sped up the golden stair
     On which the new-born ghosts make
          passing moan,
     He brought his dead—ere burial flowers
          were strewn—
Those oft-read rhymes which called her beauty
          fair.
Then stooping o'er the still form lying there
          Grey lips spake low to ears that heard
               no tone,
          As falt'ring that his songs were hers
               alone,
He placed love's gift between her cheek and
          hair.

May it not be that when his wearied soul
          Gleamed through the mists that veil the
               spirit lands,
          One broke the order of Our Lady's bands
—Clothed in sad garb with mystic aureole—
And fleeting to his side with fluttered stole,
          Held forth love's gift in passionate clasped
               hands.

Dante's Grief.

WHICH woe of all the lifelong woes that
beat
On Dante's soul lay sorest ? Not the
bread
—Tares mixed with salt—on which his
exile fed,
Not the steep stairs which scorned his weary
feet,
Nor the grim sentence, moans, and fiery heat
At hell's perse portal,—but that one dear
head,
By his most grievous sin discomforted,
Denied him salutation on the street.

Love—my heart's refuge—soft, devout, and
shy,
Loved half as maiden, rev'renced half as
queen,
If you but knew my days as coldly seen

By Michael's eyes, — stained, froward, all
  awry,
  You too would rise with proud averted
  mien,
Gather your raiment close, and pass me by.

In Memory of John Keats.

THE voice which told the soft voluptuous
  tale
 Of Madeline and love-lorn Porphyro
 Is silent now : the breezes creep and blow,
Rustling the thin brown grass with piteous
  wail
Above his grave. No grudging hearts now
  rail
  On one whose ever-spreading fame doth
  flow
 From a clear clarion, yet who long ago
Was met with scoff, and sneer, and fierce
  assail.

For now that years have blown aside all mist,
  And we appraise him at essential worth,
  He stands amongst the singers of our
  earth,
  The fairest form of that fair company
Which climbed the rugged mountain-tops,
  and kist
 The maiden lips of deathless poesy.

A Woman's Hair.

A WOMAN'S worship, Paul the Apostle
said,
    Is in her tresses, yea, her hair hath been
    The gold-fringed napkin of the Mag-
      dalene,
A stair which thrilled beneath its lover's
    tread.
In northern runes a maiden's silken head
    Hid beggar rags with purple of a queen,
    Her locks girt Galahad—as virgin clean,—
And served love's pillow for the laurelled
    dead.

Men cry abroad its virtue, Nature's art,
    Praise gloss and texture, find this colour
      fair ;
    But ah, the magic—rich, exotic, rare,—
He only knows who feels upon his heart
The treasured wonder, sacred and apart,
    Dear gage of love, a maiden's fragrant
      hair.

Prisoners of Hope.

WHAT part have I in Jesse—for the King
Scorns lukewarm service ; white of soul
are they
Who wear white raiment, victors from
the fray
Who wave His palm, and cast their crowns,
and sing.
These counted this rich life a common thing,
They wrought in sterile vineyards all
God's day,
Their sweat and blood made green a
grassless way,—
What part have I with such high following !

Ah, Lord, constrain me,—if not here and
now,
Then far through mystic æons, vast,
unknown,
Seek the faint soul and seal it for thine
own.

C

With skilled transplanting graft the barren
      bough,
Shed lustral dews, and lively heats enow,
   So this sick weed may flower before Thy
     Throne.

A Child's Dreams.

WHEN bed-time came, and childish
    prayers were prayed,
  She fell asleep, for all dear tales were
    told—
  Aladdin's lamp, the dwarf's enchanted
    gold,
And simple rhymes that please a little maid.
And now her curls—how like the soft dark
    braid
    Worn next my heart—fall, tangled fold
      in fold,
    Whilst with kissed cheeks deep pillowed
      from the cold
She dreams, watched close by love, and
    unafraid.

What silver shapes and shining fantasies
    Make night dreams strange as day
        dreams, and more fair !
    The red-cloaked witch who climbed
        Rapùnzel's hair
Haunts she this slumber ? or may now arise
    Her mother's presence stooping softly
        there,
With shadowy hair, and misty love-lit eyes ?

The Dream Child.

I.

WRAPT close in folds of ante-natal sleep,
  Thank God, dear child, that thou hast
    never been,
  Thine ears have heard not, nor thine
    eye hath seen,
Nor heart conceived life's sombre ways and
  steep.
Rest warm in soft oblivion, dreamless, deep,
  Where poppies bloom, and all the graves
    are green,
  With spotless heart, with soul unstained
    and clean,
Thank God, sleep soundly, laugh not, neither
  weep.

Better th' untimely birth, the Preacher saith,
  Than dead or living ; his the greater gain,
  For him the senses spread their snare in
    vain,

He knows not with the taking of each breath
    Life's doubtful pleasure, and its certain
       pain,
The squalid grave, the tragedy of death.

II.

And yet, perchance, were death the goal of
    life,
    Its written Finis, and the end of all,
    'Twere good to live awhile, the senses
      thrall,
And learn the worth of peace by means of
    strife.
'Twere good to woo a maiden, wed a wife,
    To pluck the common flowers that blow
      and fall,
    To dance a little in the carnival,
Perchance, perchance, were death the goal of
    life.

Ah, when th' outwearied body flags and dies,
    Might sleep and silence follow, all were
      well.
    But when the soul, reluctant, quits its
      cell,

A tragic ghost with haunted, fearful eyes—
Perchance the lurid dawn in orient skies
    May prove the smoulder of the fires of
    Hell.

The Flower Bride.

L OVE heaped the glowing harvest, argent,
　　pied,
　　　Deep coloured, richer blooms than earth
　　　　hath doled,
　　　And framed his perfect dream, shy,
　　　　silver-stoled,
To ease the heart no love had satisfied.
Whiter than lily gleamed the maiden's side,
　　　He spun her fallen hair of mary-gold,
　　　Shaped the still bosom on a rose's mould,
And wrought of scent and bud a flawless
　　Bride.

Ah, types may paint her beauty to the eyes,
　　　But flowers, though red as gold, more
　　　　pure than snow,
　　　Soft as south winds that from the spice
　　　　lands flow,
These fail to tell her thought's sweet charities,
Her heart's red love, her soul's white
　　ministries ;
　　　These have no symbol, these but one
　　　　may know.

Raymond's Mistress.

" YOU say my life is led through pleasant
ways,
By fragrant myrtles, and the ripe gold
grain,
A lily-life, untouched by care or stain,
Fulfilled with beauty, rich in love and praise.
Yet who can thread the mystic tangled maze
Which fences round a soul, or who make
plain
The barren purpose of a life-long pain
Made hid and sacred from the common gaze?"

And speaking thus she plucked her kerchief
down,
And lo, her lover saw the tender side
Fretted and wasted, " Ah mine own," she
sighed,
" If thus all eyes could pierce 'neath husk and
gown
In whose young heart would love be
deified,
Whose dainty head would men delight to
crown?"

In Memory of David Gray.

IS this the end,—a life of twenty years,
    A barren longing, and an aching heart,
    A voice unheard midst tumult of the
      mart,
A poet's raptures, and a lover's fears?
And then a white-haired mother's bitter
    tears,
    A blind surcease from God's appointed
      work,
    A grave beneath the shadow of the kirk,
Marked by the carven stone which love
    uprears.

Is this the end?—for then were living nought
    But helmless voyage, and impending
      wreck,
A school wherein the lie is ever taught,
    A painted horror for the fool to deck,
A mocking puzzle to our weary thought,
    A curse which follows at the devil's beck.

Death's Gifts.

ON hidden ways I met the Lord of Dread;
　　His breath hung frosted on the summer
　　　　heat,
　　The noontide sunshine blackened at his
　　　　feet,
And in his shadow bud and bloom lay dead.
For awe I made a darkness round my head
　　And did such rev'rence as to Death is
　　　　meet,
　　Yet all my days from bitter turned to
　　　　sweet
Within the gloom that silent Presence shed.

But when Death spake peace sank upon my
　　　　breast,
　　"Thy heart beats yet thine own for
　　　　certain days,
　　Prepare therein to meet my face with
　　　　praise,
For at my touch life's aim grows manifest,
My gifts are tireless work, or stirless rest,
　　And peace for those who wept on hidden
　　　　ways."

A Ballade of Proserpine.

1.

I BRING no gifts of spice and bread,
  Of Ophir's gold and dye of Tyre,
To deck Astarte's ivory bed
  Or heap beside her altar fire.
  No grace of love do I require,
I haunt no garish rose-hung shrine,
  But crave for ease of heart's desire
The dreamy eyes of Proserpine.

2.

Within the kingdom of the dead
  Grey Charon plies his ghostly hire,
And man and maid with soiled bare head
  Wail near the river's marsh and mire.
  Yea, never kiss, nor touch of lyre,
Nor dancing girl, nor scented wine
  May glad those souls who hymn in choir
The dreamy eyes of Proserpine.

3.

Queen of the dead whom Death's self wed,
    Whose white flesh knew no burial pyre,
On heart and brow has Lethe shed
    Forgetfulness of home and sire.
    In this thy piteous realm and dire
May peace yet cause that face to shine,
    And soothe with poppied soft strung
       wire
The dreamy eyes of Proserpine.

ENVOY.

Queen, when my fated days expire,
    Grant me to know those eyes on mine,
Eyes clear from tears, and joy, and ire,
    The dreamy eyes of Proserpine.

The Song of Her Body.

THIS is the song of her body, rose-red,
  wonderful, white,
A graft from the flora of Eden, a maid for
  her lover's delight,
A comfort of cloud from the sun, a glow of
  soft flame in the night.

God wrought her beautiful body, her limbs
  He shaped at His ease,
He graced her with colour and worship, and
  all that a lover might please,
And set His bright work 'gainst a background
  of flow'rs and flowering trees.

How may I sing of her body—her face flushes
  hot for a word,
It is hidden 'neath delicate raiment, it is sweet
  as the song of a bird
In some leafy recess of the woodland, unseen
  yet the clearlier heard.

I am bound to her beautiful body by bands of
    crepuscular hair,
It is heaped on her head as a circlet, or falls
    as a cloak she would wear,
My heart is enwebbed in its meshes, and beats
    content in the snare.

God set in her beautiful body twin casements
    to lighten the gloom,
There exquisite dreamings move whitely, like
    maids through a room,
They flicker with passionate torches, lit,
    dearest, for whom !

In the midst of her beautiful body the virginal
    bosom is spread,
It stirs to her breath and her pulses, it pillows
    one fortunate head,
And serves in a wonderful fashion for our
    love-child's daily bread.

How may I sing of her body—her face flushes
    hot for a word,
It is hidden 'neath delicate raiment, it is sweet
    as the song of a bird
In some leafy recess of the woodland, unseen
    yet the clearlier heard.

This is the song of her body, rose-red, won-
    derful, white,
A graft from the flora of Eden, a bride for
    her husband's delight,
A comfort of cloud from the sun, a warmth of
    live flame in the night.

A Spring Carol.

I HEAR the sound of growing grass,
  Of climbing sap, of bursting bud,
The wonder of the spring doth pass
  Like wine within my blood.

The trees were thick with singing birds,
  I read Dan Chaucer in my chair,
There fell across the coloured words
  The shadow of your hair.

Your voice their song, his rhyme, outsung,
    Your mouth was sweeter, love, than
      each,
The soft contralto of your tongue,
  The cadence of your speech.

Ah, if in ghostly counterfeit
  Your breathing presence came so near,
Since dreams may prove so kind a cheat
  Think how I need you, dear.

I need you as a bird the south,
  I seek with passion no man knows
The scarlet lilies of your mouth,
  Your bosom's pallid rose.

I hear the sound of growing grass,
  Of climbing sap, of bursting bud,
The magic of the spring doth pass
  Like wine within my blood.

Then haste, dear love, like sudden spring
  O'er stable lands, o'er shifting sea,
Most sweet, most fair that welcoming
  When hands are clasped with thee.

Prelude to a St. Dorothy.

I LEARNED this legend from a silent
    tongue
  In simple days when faith was clear and
    glad,
I cannot speak the spell its beauty flung
    About one dreamy lad.

It haunted all the passage of my youth,
    A mystic shadow moving near to me,
A Roman lady, witness to Christ's truth,
    God's maiden, Dorothy.

And now in manhood if I dare rehearse
    This saintly legend of dim Pagan days,
May her bright presence lighten my poor
    verse,
    Refine it to her praise.

May she who sent Theophilus the flowers
  Grant in this rhyme some fragrance may
      arise,
Perfume of roses from uncankered bowers,
  Rich strays of Paradise.

Grant also, lady, some prevailing prayer,
  That after penal cleansing, by Christ's
      grace,
I too may tread those orchard gardens fair,
  And bow before thy face.

Old French.

IF Love should pass with trailing wing !
I may not sleep for sorrowing.

In dreamless watches of the night
Love's parted presence seeks my sight.

I left my bed at dawn of day
And took my cloak of fur and grey.

In orchard glooms birds sought their mate
I entered by a wicket gate.

And lo, the lark and nightingale
Told to my heart a wondrous tale.

For thus they sang that matin tide,
"My true love hastens to my side.

E'en now his boat of painted wood
Beats with swift oars the Seine to flood.

Her satin sails spread fold on fold,
With silken cordage manifold,
And rudder of the beaten gold.

Near ivory masts her sailors stand,
Fair men and strangers to this land.

One wears the broidered fleur de lys,
The King of France's son is he.

And eager, near the Prince's side
My true love hastens to his bride."

Sonnet.

(After Baudelaire.)

IN far south lands made sweet with fragrant
　　balms
　　I knew, beneath the shade of purpled
　　　trees
And drowsy stillness of the drooping palms,
　　Afar from towns, withdrawn in slothful
　　　ease,
A Creole lady.　Pale her tint, but warm,
　　With soft brown skin, and nobly carried
　　　head,
With tranquil smile, and dainty slender form,
　　Assured calm eyes, and supple springy
　　　tread.

If ever, madam, fate shall shape your ways
    To glorious France, your grace—which
        nothing lacks
        To flash the jewel of some ancient
           seat—
        Within the shadows of your sure
           retreat
Will cause a thousand sonnets in its praise,
    And make our hearts more humble than
        your blacks.

Exotic Perfume.

(AFTER BAUDELAIRE.)

IN autumn twilight, when with fast closed
  eyes
   I breathe the fragrance of thy fervent
     breast,
About me spreads a reach of changeless skies,
   And sunlit dazzling shores in happy rest.
A drowsy isle, the dainty forcing place
   Of luscious fruits, and strange gigantic
     trees,
The sultry dwelling of a slender race
   Whose girls are frank and lightsome as
     the breeze.

Led thus by dreams towards these sunset climes,
   I gaze upon a crowded port, a throng
   Of masts and sails, an open windswept
     sea,
Whilst from the land the perfume of the
     limes
   Makes sweet the air, and comes across to
     me
Blent with the chorus of a sailor's song.

D

An Old Goldsmith.

(From the French of Heredia.)

I HANDLED brush and graver with more
    ease,
      More deftness, than all Masters of the
        Guild,
      In jewelled work my subtle brain was
        skilled,
I shaped the vase, and wrought its storied
    frieze.
Now, silver and enamel fail to please,
      For there I traced—so my snared soul
        hath willed—
      No sacred Rood, no Deacon Lawrence
        grilled,
But vine-girt gods, or Danae's gold-clasped
    knees.

To Hell's own service my red forge inlaid
With fair devices some rich rufflers blade,
    Till deep in pride my part of Life is lost.

Thus seeing I grow fearful, and am old,
E'er death may come and falling dark enfold
    I chase a golden monstrance for the Host.

The Chatelaine.

(FROM THE FRENCH OF RICHEPIN.)

WITHIN a chamber dim with tapestry,
  Stiff in her long straight girdle edged
    with fur
  And steeple cap, the Chatelaine broods
    there,
The linen veil falls whitely to her knee.
She fingers at the rebeck listlessly
  And dreams of him who plighted troth
    with her,
  He fights to gain Christ's holy sepulchre
In pagan lands beyond the weary sea.

When he shall come to wed the maid he
  wooed
And pluck the lily of her maidenhood
  What priest may tell, what subtle wizard
    know ?
  But should he die before the felon foe
True to her faithful promise, chaste and good,
  No kiss shall warm her bosom's virgin
    snow.

CPSIA information can be obtained
at www.ICGtesting.com
Printed in the USA
BVHW081339200921
617096BV00003B/365

9 783348 063883